Ibrahim Khan

and the Mystery of the Roaring Lion

For Ibrahim, Nur-ul-Huda, Sulaiman & their Papa.
Couldn't have done it without you!

Ibrahim Khan

and the Mystery of the Roaring Lion

FARHEEN KHAN

THE ISLAMIC FOUNDATION

MUSLIM CHILDREN'S LIBRARY

IBRAHIM KHAN SERIES

Ibrahim Khan and the Mystery of the Roaring Lion
Author Farheen Khan
Editor Farah Alvi
Illustrator Sharelle (Shahada) Haqq
Cover/Book design & typeset Nasir Cadir
Coordinator Anwar Cara

Published by
THE ISLAMIC FOUNDATION
Markfield Conference Centre, Ratby Lane, Markfield
Leicestershire, LE67 9SY, United Kingdom
E-mail: publications@islamic-foundation.com
Website: www.islamic-foundation.com

Quran House, P.O. Box 30611, Nairobi, Kenya

P.M.B. 3193, Kano, Nigeria

Distributed by
Kube Publishing Ltd.
Tel: +44(01530) 249230, Fax: +44(01530) 249656
E-mail: info@kubepublishing.com
Website: www.kubepublishing.com

A Cataloguing-in-Publication Data record for this book is available from the British Library

ISBN 9780860374671

CONTENTS

CHAPTER ONE

A New Case

"Ring, ring... Ring, ring"

"Hello?" Ibrahim answered.

"Ibrahim? Ibrahim Khan?" asked the low voice on the other end.

"Yeah, it's me. Who's calling?"

"Yusuf Ali, from school," came the nervous reply. "I... I heard you do detective work."

"That's right," replied Ibrahim. "A dollar a case if it's just me or two if I'll need the help of my assistant, Zayn."

"I'll give you five if you get started right away," Yusuf offered.

"Wow, if you're sure. Where would you like to meet?"

"My place," Yusuf answered, "and hurry!"

After making a quick call to his cousin Zayn, Ibrahim ran to his room to change. Pulling on an orange t-shirt and jeans, he checked the time. It was 4:45, almost time for *Asr* prayer and Ibrahim knew he had to be home before *Maghrib*.

Ibrahim, Zayn and Yusuf were all in third grade together, but the Khan boys, as their teacher Mrs. Morris liked to call them, didn't know Yusuf very well. He was the quietest boy in class, maybe even the school. No one had ever been to his house, but they all knew where he lived, the large grey brick house at the end of Stanley Lane. It was larger than the other houses in the neighbourhood and had a lot of great climbing trees. In the Autumn, when all the trees began shedding their colourful leaves, Yusuf's house was the envy of all the neighbourhood kids.

🐾

As Ibrahim rode his old yellow bike towards Yusuf's house, he could see Zayn waiting for him on his shiny red bike, at the end of the long driveway.

"Do you have rocket boosters on your bike?" Ibrahim yelled as he came closer. "How'd you get here so fast?"

"I can just pedal faster than you, that's all," Zayn shrugged.

"Don't you think it's a little suspicious you became a faster pedaller right after you got that new bike last Eid?" grumbled Ibrahim.

Zayn just laughed as he followed his cousin to the enormous front doors.

"Have you ever been to Yusuf's house before?" asked Zayn.

"No, I don't think anyone in our class has," Ibrahim answered.

"It's kind of a shame to have so many great climbing trees but no kids around to climb them," Zayn commented. "Why do you think Yusuf doesn't have anyone over?"

"I don't know, maybe he's just shy," Ibrahim suggested.

"Yeah, maybe…" answered Zayn. Neither boy noticed the dark pair of eyes peeking out of a nearby hedge.

CHAPTER TWO

🐾 🐾 🐾

A Lion in Your WHAT???

Ibrahim was about to ring the doorbell when the front door flew open.

"Took you guys long enough!"

Ibrahim and Zayn looked up to see a rather annoyed-looking Yusuf standing in the doorway. "Well, don't just stand there, get in!"

"Right," said Ibrahim.

"*Assalamu 'Alaykum*," mumbled Zayn as he entered the house.

As Yusuf led the boys up to his room, Ibrahim could tell that like him, Zayn was also feeling uncomfortable.

"You have a nice house, *Masha'Allah*," Ibrahim politely commented. Getting no reply the boys quietly followed Yusuf into his room. The room, a little bigger than Ibrahim's, looked like a tornado had just swept through. The carpet, which looked like it was probably white at some time, could barely be seen under comic books, Transformers, cars and lots and lots of Lego. As the boys made room for themselves around the room, Ibrahim took out a notebook and pencil.

"Listen guys," Yusuf sighed. "I'm sorry if I seem uptight, it's just that... well, this is really serious."

"It's okay, just tell us what happened from the beginning," said Ibrahim.

"It all started last week. I had just brushed my teeth and was making room on the floor for my prayer-mat so I could pray *'Isha'*, when I heard hyenas laughing in the back yard," Yusuf explained as he nervously fidgeted with his hands. Ibrahim and Zayn raised an eyebrow at each other but let Yusuf continue.

"Well, I was a little freaked out but I started praying anyway. I was about half way through my prayer when I heard it. The blood-chilling sound of a ferocious roaring lion! In my backyard!!" yelled Yusuf, with a frantic look in his eyes. "It took all my strength to finish my prayer before I ran to my parents' room. My dad checked in the yard with a flashlight but he didn't find anything."

At first Ibrahim thought Yusuf was crying, but he quickly realized the noise was coming from Zayn, who was trying very hard not to laugh! Glaring at Zayn, Ibrahim turned his attention back to Yusuf.

"So… you're saying there were hyenas and umm, a lion in your back yard?"

Ibrahim scribbled some notes, trying hard to be professional but it was difficult with Zayn in the same room. "Err, Zayn, why don't you take a look around the yard for clues while I continue with Yusuf?"

Zayn nodded, without saying a word, and headed out of the room.

"Okay Yusuf, I'm going to be honest with you," Ibrahim began. "It's not that I don't believe you, but

I'm pretty sure there are no hyenas and definitely no lions loose on Stanley Lane."

Just then a loud burst of laughter came in through the window, a laugh they both knew belonged to Zayn.

"You guys don't believe me!" Yusuf shouted. "I knew this was a mistake! First my parents don't believe me and now you two. I know what I heard," Yusuf finished in a whisper.

"I believe you! Well, I believe that you believe you heard hyenas and a lion," Ibrahim tried to explain. "Now it's my job to find out what really happened last week. Is this the only time you've heard strange things in the night?"

"It was," answered Yusuf, "until two nights ago. For the past two nights I've been hearing the lion again."

"No hyenas?" asked Ibrahim

"Nope," Yusuf answered, "just lions."

CHAPTER THREE

Day One of the Lion Hunt

After a quick discussion with Zayn, Ibrahim called home to get permission to spend the night at Yusuf's house. Zayn's job was to research the surrounding woods both on-line and in his parent's vast library. The boys rode home together since Ibrahim still had to go home and get his things. His dad had agreed to bring him back later that evening.

"Do you want me to drop off my fishing net?" Zayn asked his cousin.

"You want me to catch a lion with a fishing net?" Ibrahim replied, slightly out of breath. "Besides, I don't plan on catching anything tonight."

"You don't?" Zayn asked, a little surprised.

"No, tonight I'll be a fly on the wall. I want to hear what Yusuf's been hearing," Ibrahim explained. As he wiped the sweat off his forehead, he looked over at Zayn's new bike. "Why is it you're pedalling less than me but going the same speed?"

"If the famous detective Ibrahim Khan can't figure it out, how am I supposed to know?" Zayn teased as he rode off to the right, heading to his house.

Ibrahim just shook his head as he continued up the street deep in thought about Yusuf, lions and hyenas.

🐾

"Call me in the morning when you want to be picked up," Ibrahim's dad told him, as he helped him carry his sleeping bag to Yusuf's front door.

"Thanks *Abbu*!" Ibrahim said, as he waved from the front porch. Tomorrow was Saturday and Ibrahim knew he'd be missing his mamma's famous waffles in the morning.

"Oh well," he shrugged. "Being a detective isn't always easy."

Once again, before Ibrahim had the chance to ring the door bell, the door was opened by Yusuf.

"*Assalamu 'Alaykum*," Yusuf greeted Ibrahim with a small smile.

"*Wa'alaykum as-Salam*," Ibrahim answered.

"So you're Ibrahim, eh?" came a voice from the kitchen. Ibrahim looked over and saw Yusuf's big brother Kamran sitting at the kitchen table eating a bowl of ice cream.

"Just ignore him," Yusuf whispered, as he carried Ibrahim's sleeping bag in.

"I heard from lil' Yusuf here that you're going to catch the big bad giraffe in our yard," Kamran teased, as he started laughing loudly.

Yusuf quickly dragged Ibrahim the rest of the way up before he had a chance to reply.

"I guess he doesn't believe you either?" Ibrahim asked, as Yusuf closed the door behind them.

"No, no one does," Yusuf sighed. "But you'll see for yourself tonight. Then you can tell everyone I'm telling the truth!"

Yusuf had cleared up a little and there was now enough room for Ibrahim to set up his sleeping bag under the large window that overlooked the back yard. He pulled out his brown sack which carried all the surveillance equipment he'd need for the night.

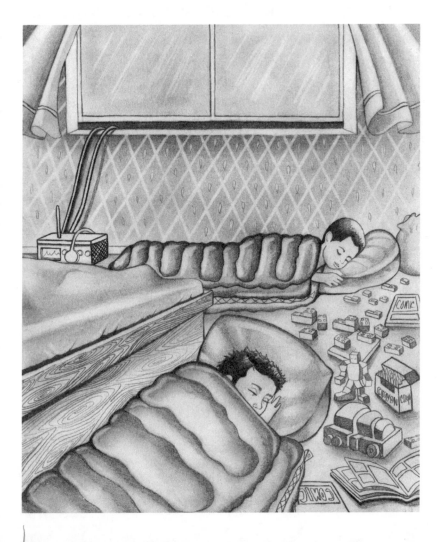

"You don't mind if I leave the window open a crack do you?" Ibrahim asked. "I'm going to have to run a few wires through the window," he explained.

"Do whatever you need to," said Yusuf. "Say, is that your famous brown sack?" he asked. "I heard the boys at school talking about it. One of the boys in grade two thought it was magic!"

"It's a special padded bag actually, not magical at all," replied Ibrahim. "I'll have to ask you not to look in it though, a detective has to have some secrets," he said with a smile.

Ibrahim continued to set up the delicate-looking equipment both in Yusuf's room and out on his window sill, while Yusuf got ready for *'Isha'*. As the boys prayed Ibrahim thought he heard something outside but ignored it and continued his *salah*.

CHAPTER FOUR

The Midnight Visitor

As Ibrahim lay in his sleeping bag under the window, the only sound he could hear was Yusuf's steady breathing. Yusuf had asked Ibrahim to wake him up if anything happened and Ibrahim had agreed. However, there were no laughing hyenas or roaring lions. It was starting to get late but Ibrahim stayed awake, waiting for the lion to return.

It was almost midnight when Ibrahim first heard the sounds of hyenas in the back yard and they were laughing! He quietly slipped out of his sleeping bag and peered into the yard. Less than a minute later he heard a loud thunderous roar! He grabbed his binoculars and held them against the window. There was definitely something out there, something big!

"Yusuf!" Ibrahim called in an urgent whisper. "Yusuf, get up! The lion's back!!"

Leaving the window Ibrahim went to shake Yusuf awake.

"Wha—?" Yusuf answered in a groggy voice. "What's going on?" he yelled.

"Come see for yourself," Ibrahim said, as he rushed back to the window. Now fully awake, Yusuf quickly joined him.

"Pass me the binoculars Ibrahim! I want to see! Let me see, let me see!" he pleaded.

"Shhh! You're making too much noise!" Ibrahim warned, as he tried to find the figures he had seen earlier. After a minute or two of searching Ibrahim let out a loud groan.

"They're gone," he moaned.

"They?" Yusuf asked. "You mean there was more than one lion?"

"I… I don't know. There was definitely more than one, but I didn't get a good enough look," Ibrahim explained.

"What do you mean, isn't this your job? I mean, you are a detective aren't you?!" Yusuf asked in disbelief.

"It was dark, so I didn't really see much. I'm sorry," said Ibrahim. He was frustrated and didn't want to tell Yusuf it was his fault for making too much noise. "Listen, let's just get some sleep. Hopefully, I caught something on my surveillance equipment. Zayn and I can check it out tomorrow. I don't think there'll be any more lions tonight. I'll have to spend another night here, but this time with Zayn."

"Sure," Yusuf answered with a yawn as he got back into bed.

"And Yusuf?" Ibrahim continued.

"Yeah?"

"Tomorrow night it might be better if I wake you up after we catch what's out there," Ibrahim suggested.

"Hmm," Yusuf replied, as his steady breathing quickly turned into light snoring.

CHAPTER FIVE

Day Two of the Lion Hunt

Ibrahim spent the early morning hours after *Fajr* looking for prints in the back yard. Though he wasn't sure who the culprit was, he had a theory. He'd have to wait till nightfall to prove it. After a delicious breakfast of pancakes with the yummiest syrup he'd ever had, Ibrahim called his dad to come pick him up. He had packed most of his things but left his sleeping bag and toothbrush behind. He had a busy day ahead of him which included an afternoon nap. Ibrahim knew he needed to be extra alert tonight.

"Thanks for breakfast Yusuf," said Ibrahim. "The pancakes were delicious."

"You're welcome," Yusuf replied. "We have a couple of maple trees in the back. We collected sap from it last spring to make that syrup."

"That's really cool!" Ibrahim exclaimed. "You should tell Mrs. Morris, I'm sure the kids in class would love to help you guys turn the sap into syrup. It would be like a field trip!"

Ibrahim watched as a look of horror passed over Yusuf's face.

"Bu-but all those people in, in *my* back yard," Yusuf stammered. "Climbing on *my* trees, playing in *my* tree house. No, I don't think it would be a good idea."

"It would be so cool though," Ibrahim explained. "Can you imagine how much fun it would be with the whole class in your yard!?"

"No," Yusuf answered in a small voice. "I can't."

Ibrahim thought Yusuf looked sad, but he couldn't understand why. The sound of honking broke up the conversation. Ibrahim's dad was there to pick him up. After a quick good-bye Ibrahim promised Yusuf he'd return that evening.

🐾

After a quick shower Ibrahim headed off to Zayn's house. The boys analyzed the recordings from Yusuf's window sill as Ibrahim told Zayn all about the night's events and Zayn told him what he'd found during his research.

"You should have just left Yusuf sleeping," Zayn suggested.

"I know," Ibrahim agreed. "But what's done is done. We need to pack the brown sack for tonight. We'll need both image and sound recording equipment as well as a really, really big net."

Zayn looked surprised but didn't question his cousin as the boys headed down to the garage for a net. Zayn's dad loved to fish so he had many nets of different sizes. The boys were allowed to borrow what they needed as long as they put it back where they found it.

Both the boys' parents supported their detective work as long as they kept their grades up and let their parents know where they'd be.

"I looked in our library and on my dad's computer to see if there was any information about the woods behind Yusuf's house," said Zayn. "But couldn't find much."

"Did you find anything at all?" asked Ibrahim.

"Just a couple of old newspaper articles. The only wildlife mentioned in them were squirrels, chipmunks and an occasional skunk," Zayn explained. "The closest lion or hyena to Stanley Lane is a two and a half hour drive away, at the zoo!"

"That's what I figured," said Ibrahim. "But it's good to be sure."

Ibrahim and Zayn worked in the garage tying small weights around the edges of the net.

"Have you asked your parents about staying at Yusuf's house tonight?" Ibrahim asked.

"Yup!" Zayn answered. "Did you let Yusuf know I'd be spending the night?"

"Yeah, he knows," Ibrahim answered.

"Do you think I should apologize to him?" Zayn asked. "You know, for laughing at him and all."

"That would be nice," said Ibrahim. "It's really not a good idea to laugh at our clients," he added, grinning.

"I know, I know," said Zayn. "But come on Ibrahim, hyenas and lions wandering our neighbourhood?!"

Both boys burst out laughing.

CHAPTER SIX

The Cat's in the Bag

It was 8 in the evening when Ibrahim's dad dropped the boys off at Yusuf's house. They set up the large net, a few powerful lights and their recording equipment in the back yard before ringing the doorbell. Once the boys had prayed *'Isha'* they began to prepare for bed. This time Zayn rolled out his sleeping bag under the window while Ibrahim's sleeping bag remained packed by the door.

"Aren't you going to sleep here too?" Yusuf asked Ibrahim.

"No," said Ibrahim. "Tonight I'll be sleeping in your tree house."

"What?!" yelled Yusuf. "It's not safe! What if – what if they get you in the night?"

"Don't worry," Ibrahim tried to reassure him. "Zayn will be watching me from inside and can get your dad if I need help," he explained.

Yusuf still didn't look happy about it, but finally agreed.

The crescent moon rose high in the night sky, bathing the yard in its pale light. As Ibrahim snuggled deeper into his sleeping bag, he checked his watch for the third time. It was only 9:30. Still early he thought. His eyes had adjusted to the dim light, so he could clearly see most of the back yard. There was nothing to do now but wait. Even though he couldn't see Zayn without his binoculars, Ibrahim knew Zayn was watching him, ready to help. An hour passed with nothing but the sound of an owl hooting and the neighbour's dog barking.

Ibrahim had almost dozed off when he heard a rustling sound nearby. Silently creeping to the edge of the tree house doorway, Ibrahim lay ready and waiting. Holding up two fingers to Zayn, he signalled him to stand by. Then he heard the sounds of twigs snapping as he grabbed the net.

"Do you think those nosy detectives are back?" asked a hushed deep voice.

"Nah, they probably thought Yusuf was going crazy like everyone else," whispered a softer voice. "I still feel bad, you said this was supposed to be a joke but I think he's really scared."

"Well it's his fault for being so selfish. Now come on Mariam play the tape so we can get out of here," demanded the deeper voice.

"Mariam?" Ibrahim wondered. "Could it be Mariam Hamid from class? It did sound a lot like her," he thought. Ibrahim signalled Zayn with all five fingers just as the sound of a ferocious lion split the night air. Dropping the net over the culprits Ibrahim flicked the switch to turn on the flood lights.

"What! What's going on?!" demanded the deeper voice.

"Ahhh!" screamed the voice Ibrahim now knew was Mariam's. "I'm sorry, I'm sorry, I didn't mean to! He made me do it! It was just supposed to be a joke!"

"Shhh!" said the deeper voice.

As Ibrahim came down the ladder he couldn't help but chuckle at the scene in front of him. Tangled in a heap of arms, legs and sturdy fishing net was Mariam Hamid and her older brother Omar Hamid. Mariam was in third grade with Ibrahim, Zayn and Yusuf while her older brother was in tenth grade with Yusuf's brother Kamran. As the back porch lights turned on, out rushed Zayn, Yusuf and Yusuf's dad. Mariam let out a loud sob at the sight of the three. The moment of truth had arrived.

CHAPTER SEVEN

Confessions

"What's going on here?!" demanded Yusuf's dad. However, before Ibrahim could explain, Mariam cut in.

"I'm sorry Mr. Ali," she sobbed. "Please don't call the police!"

A moment later a sleepy-looking Kamran stepped out of the house.

"Omar? What are you doing in my yard?" he asked, rubbing the sleep from his eyes. Omar didn't answer as he lay tangled on the grass.

"Why don't we go inside?" Ibrahim suggested.

Mr. Ali nodded as he stepped back inside. The Khan boys began to free Omar and Mariam from the fishing net, as Yusuf and Kamran followed their dad into the house. Once everyone had assembled around the kitchen table, Ibrahim noticed how pale Yusuf looked.

"It's okay Yusuf, it's over now," Ibrahim said, trying to comfort him.

"Why? Why would they do that to me?" Yusuf whispered.

At first no one answered. Then Ibrahim saw Omar's face twist in anger.

"It's all your fault!" he yelled. But to everyone's surprise he wasn't yelling at Yusuf, he was yelling at Kamran.

"What! What did I do!" Kamran yelled back.

Omar stood, shaking with anger.

"Don't you remember when we were in Mrs. Morris' class?" Omar began. "It was the same thing then. You never let anyone play with your 'cool toys', never let us come over and didn't even let us climb the trees in your yard. It's not like you planted them there!"

No one dared to speak as Omar continued.

"I remember when your dad built that tree house. You bragged to the whole class about it, but we all knew we'd never be allowed near it. Everyone knew how selfish you were. When Mariam came home from school last month complaining about how your little brother wouldn't share his markers when she had forgotten hers, because he thought she would ruin them, I had had enough. It was time for revenge!"

Omar turned his attention to Yusuf who seemed to tremble under his glare. "What makes you guys think you're better than the rest of us? Why is it so hard for you to share?" he demanded.

"Enough!" Kamran shouted as he too stood, but instead of facing Omar he stood looking out of the window by the backyard. "It's not Yusuf's fault," he spoke in a whisper. "It's me, I'm the one who doesn't like to share. I know it's not right, but I just can't, I'm afraid to… It started after Yusuf was born, I was always scared he would take my things and break them. Whenever he came near my things I'd yell at him. Eventually I couldn't share with anyone, not even my friends. Yusuf learned not to share… from

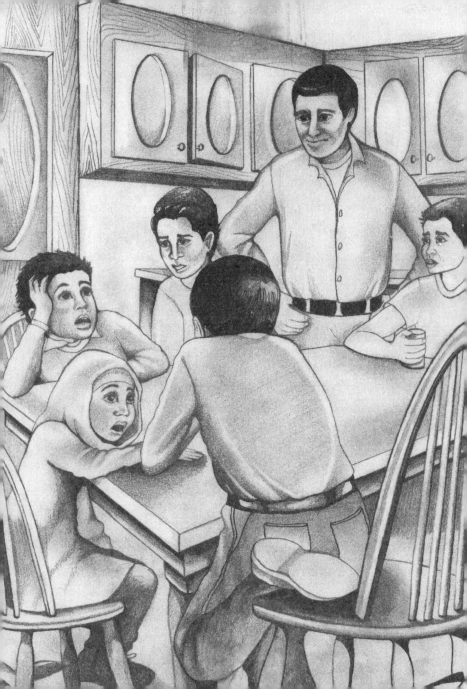

me." Kamran turned to face Omar as he continued. "But you had no right to scare my little brother."

As the boys fell silent, Mr. Ali addressed both his sons.

"Boys, I'm really disappointed in you. Your mother and I have always thought that by giving regularly to charity ourselves, the two of you would also learn to be generous," he said. "Omar, I've known you for a long time and know you're a good boy, but jealousy can make people do things they wouldn't normally do. Scaring Yusuf like that wasn't very nice."

"No it wasn't, Mr. Ali," replied Omar, in a much calmer voice. "And I'm sorry. I figured if Kamran and Yusuf wouldn't let us play in their yard, then they shouldn't get to play in it either. And that was very, um—selfish of me."

Omar looked down at his hands. "I'm sorry I scared you Yusuf. Mariam, I'm sorry I dragged you into this. The markers really weren't a big deal. I… I was jealous and wanted to get back at Kamran, through Yusuf."

Kamran was the first to extend his hand to Omar.

"It's okay man, we all make mistakes," he said, with a smile.

Soon all the boys shook hands and forgave each other.

"I have a question," said Mariam. "How did you guys figure it out? I've been snooping around here quite a lot and I was pretty sure you guys didn't believe Yusuf's story. When did you realize there were no wild animals around?"

Everyone turned to look at Ibrahim for an answer, but he just shook his head.

"Sorry Mariam, that's between me and my brown sack. I'd be out of business if I gave all my secrets away," Ibrahim replied with a smile.

CHAPTER EIGHT

Another Case Solved

Since it was so late Ibrahim and Zayn decided to spend the rest of the night at Yusuf's house while Mr. Ali walked Omar and Mariam home. After *Fajr* prayer the boys began to dismantle and pack up their equipment.

"You're really not going to tell anyone how you figured it out?" Zayn asked Ibrahim as they unhooked the flood lights.

"You know you're my partner Zayn," Ibrahim answered. "What do you want to know?"

"Well, I still don't know exactly when you realized you were catching a couple of kids and not a wild animal," said Zayn.

"Do you remember the first time we came to Yusuf's house?" Ibrahim asked. "I had sent you in the yard so I could discuss the case with Yusuf in peace."

"How could I forget?" Zayn said a little sheepishly.

"Well," Ibrahim continued, "when you burst out laughing you were very close to Yusuf's bedroom window. I knew it was you laughing, but it got me thinking. If someone, not quite so loud and a little further away were laughing in the back yard, it could quite easily be mistaken for the sounds a hyena makes."

Zayn nodded in understanding.

"So when we were adding the weights to the net, you knew we'd be catching kids?" he asked. "Why didn't you tell me?"

"I wasn't totally sure until I played the tape from two nights ago again at home. We were too busy talking in your lab and we missed something."

"I thought there was nothing but the sound of wind blowing and that annoying dog next door on that tape," said Zayn.

"So did I, at first." Ibrahim explained. "But when I was listening to it at home I'm sure I heard a conversation. A whispered one, and it was kind of far from where the mike was set up, but definitely a human conversation."

Once the boys were inside they heard Yusuf call them from the kitchen.

"Up for some pancakes guys?" he asked.

"If it's with some of your homemade syrup, definitely!" Zayn replied. "Ibrahim told me all about your maple trees."

As Ibrahim filled his glass with cold milk he noticed Yusuf looked a little anxious.

"You okay Yusuf?" he asked.

"Yeah," said Yusuf. "I was just thinking about what you said, you know, about the class coming here for a field trip. Do you really think Mrs. Morris would let us?"

"Well, there's only one way to find out," Ibrahim answered. "I can talk to her on Monday if you'd like."

"That's okay, I'll talk to her myself."

Yusuf chuckled at the Khan boys' surprised faces. "I'm trying to make some changes, and the first thing on the list is 'talk to people,'" Yusuf declared.

Ibrahim, Zayn and Yusuf spent the next hour eating pancakes dripping with sweet golden maple syrup, laughing and chatting like old friends.

As the boys headed home, Yusuf paid them $2.50 each. Once he got home Ibrahim put his earnings straight into his tomato-soup can, which he used to save up for a new bike. He had a long way to go before he could get the new ZX50, but every case got him a little closer. It was one model up from Zayn's bike the ZX45 and had a few new features that would come in handy when he'd need to get somewhere in a hurry.

"Then I'll be faster than Zayn again," Ibrahim thought to himself as he took out his homework. Opening his maths text book, he wondered when he'd get his next case. "I hope I don't have to wait too long," he thought, as he began working on his fractions.

Glossary

Salah
Prayer.

Fajr
Prayer before sunrise.

'Asr
Late afternoon prayer.

Maghrib
Prayer immediately after sunset.

Assalamu 'Alaykum
Peace be on you. (Muslim greeting)

Wa'alaykum as-Salam
And on you be peace. (reply to greeting)

Masha'Allah
As Allah wills.

Abbu
Father.

Quiz

What is the name of the street Yusuf lives on?

In which season did Yusuf collect sap from the maple trees?

What is Ibrahim saving for?

What animal sound does Ibrahim record during his first night at Yusuf's house?

When did Zayn get his bike, the ZX45?

What would you have done differently if you were Ibrahim Khan solving the case of The Roaring Lion?

What did Kamran learn about himself at the end of the story?

What was Omar sorry about?

Hidden Words

Can you find the following words hidden in the grid on page 51?

- Detectives
- Kamran
- Tree House
- Roaring Lion
- Yusuf Ali
- Mariam
- Laughing Hyenas
- Zayn
- Omar
- Ibrahim
- Brown Sack
- Rocket Boosters
- Khan Boys
- Maple Syrup
- Stanley Lane

S	T	A	N	L	E	Y	L	A	N	E	E	R	S	R
A	R	O	M	A	R	N	M	F	I	D	R	T	F	O
M	E	B	F	U	U	B	L	C	U	I	O	Y	G	C
N	E	D	A	G	B	R	O	W	N	S	A	C	K	K
W	H	G	R	H	Y	V	K	D	Y	O	R	U	A	E
A	O	I	H	I	B	R	A	H	I	M	I	I	M	T
Q	U	J	E	N	T	C	J	I	T	P	N	O	R	B
A	S	K	E	G	R	X	H	S	R	M	G	P	A	O
R	E	L	N	H	E	Z	H	A	E	N	L	M	N	O
B	F	P	D	Y	U	S	U	F	A	L	I	A	D	S
V	D	E	T	E	C	T	I	V	E	S	O	R	F	T
C	Z	A	Y	N	W	Q	G	Q	W	B	N	I	G	E
X	D	K	H	A	N	B	O	Y	S	J	E	A	H	R
Z	S	V	B	S	J	H	U	D	A	V	W	M	J	S
M	A	P	L	E	S	Y	R	U	P	C	Q	L	K	A

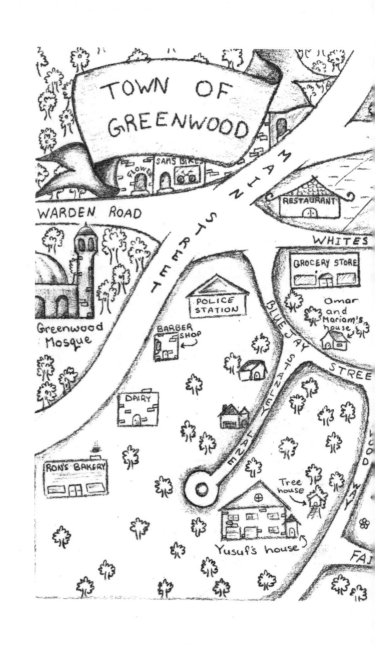

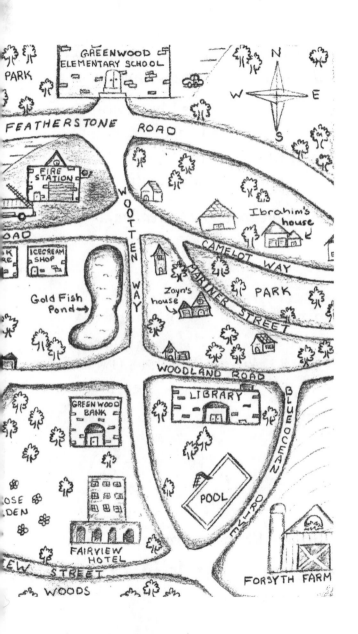

*Keep a look out for two more exciting
adventures by Ibrahim Khan ...*

- Ibrahim Khan and the Mystery of the Haunted Lake
- Ibrahim Khan and the Mystery of the Lightening Hovercraft

and more to follow thereafter....

Ibrahim Khan and the Mystery of the Haunted Lake FARHEEN KHAN	**Ibrahim Khan** and the Mystery of the Lightening Hovercraft FARHEEN KHAN

Visit Ibrahim Khan and friends on-line at

www.Ibrahim-khan.com